THE ADVENTURES OF
RALPHIE THE ROACH

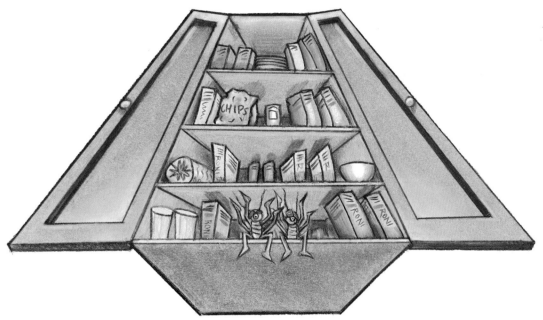

PAULINA PORIZKOVA AND JOANNE RUSSELL
ILLUSTRATED BY ADAM OTCASEK

DOUBLEDAY
NEW YORK   LONDON   TORONTO   SYDNEY   AUCKLAND

PUBLISHED BY DOUBLEDAY
a division of Bantam Doubleday Dell Publishing Group, Inc.
666 Fifth Avenue, New York, New York 10103

DOUBLEDAY
and the portrayal of an anchor with a dolphin
are trademarks of Doubleday, a division of
Bantam Doubleday Dell Publishing Group, Inc.

DESIGNED BY PETER R. KRUZAN

Library of Congress Cataloging-in-Publication Data
Porizkova, Paulina.
The adventures of Ralphie the Roach / by Paulina Porizkova, Joanne
Russell ; illustrations by Adam Otcasek.
p.   cm.
Summary: When humans Henry and Hedda Horrible move into the empty
house where Ralphie the Roach lives with his family and friends, the
roaches of the world are summoned to help save the day.
[1. Cockroaches—Fiction.]   I. Russell, Joanne.   II. Otcasek,
Adam, ill.   III. Title.
PZ7.P79925Ad   1992
[E]—dc20   91-34738   CIP   AC
ISBN 0-385-42402-7

To my boys, Derek, Eron and Jachym.

—Paulina Porizkova

•

To my mother, Anne, and my brother, Niall.

—Joanne Russell

•

To my grandfather, George Campbell.

—Adam Otcasek

ROACHTOWN is a small village behind a cupboard shelf in a big empty house in New York City. Ralphie lives there with his mom Rose and his dad Ronald in a nice, roomy crack in the wall. Ralphie is seven years old and has lived in Roachtown all of his life. His parents and grandparents have lived there all of their lives, too. In fact, Ralphie often sits with his grandfather, the sound of the boats in the distance, and listens wide-eyed to the story of how, very long ago, a Spanish ship called *tooBIGtoBEaCANOE* was sunk by a pirate ship. Lots of roaches escaped along with hundreds of Ralphie's relatives and sailed to America on a pirate's wooden leg, landing safely in New York City.

T H E first house his relatives came across was at 7 State Street where Ralphie's family still lives hundreds of years later. Their little wooden house is the only one left. Tall, modern skyscrapers surround it and it seems to have been forgotten. A small park with red wooden benches sits across from the house and PEOPLE come there every day to enjoy the view of the harbor and the ships.

T H E roaches of Roachtown work in the park every night after the PEOPLE have left, gathering all the crumbs from food PEOPLE have dropped—pieces of hot dogs, sandwiches, pretzels and doughnuts. This way the roaches clean the park and also collect all kinds of good food to bring back home.

Once Ralphie's parents even found a jelly bean and all the Roachtown kids shared it. It was the best thing Ralphie had ever tasted and he longed for his parents to find another one.

L I F E in Roachtown was peaceful and happy. No one ever came to the little forgotten house, until one terrible day. Amid a lot of banging and clunking two awful **PEOPLE** moved into the roaches' house at 7 State Street. Hedda and Helmut Horrible were a truly nasty and despicable couple. These people hated cleaning and washing and as soon as they arrived they began to mess everything up. If Hedda or Helmut had macaroni and cheese for dinner you could be sure that little macaronis were scattered everywhere. Some would even get stuck to the Horribles' clothes for *weeks*.

T H E roaches of Roachtown had always tried to keep the house clean, but now it was a terrible mess. Worst of all, the Horribles were **PEOPLE** and everyone knows **PEOPLE** don't *like* cockroaches. The Horribles talked about roaches and said they were very ugly. They didn't want to have any in their house. Of course they didn't know about Roachtown because the roaches came out only at night when the Horribles were fast asleep.

Ralphie had seen **PEOPLE** only in pictures but he decided they were a strange-looking bunch, even stranger than a dog who once wandered into the house.

RALPHIE and his best friend Conrad went to a small school along with all the other children in Roachtown. Ralphie and Conrad liked school, but they would have liked it much better if the three roach brothers Spit, Slime and Splat had gone to a different school. They missed classes, they never did their homework and they always picked on little kids.

Ralphie tried to pay attention in class, but Spit, Slime and Splat were always chewing gum, talking to each other and throwing the chewed gumballs at their classmates. Spit, Slime and Splat bragged that they had been to the Horribles' kitchen in broad daylight!

O N E Saturday Ralphie and Conrad decided to go out and play. They were pretending Conrad was a **PEOPLE**, as he chased Ralphie all around Roachtown. Suddenly they noticed Spit, Slime and Splat watching them.

"Hey, dudes, what's up?" Spit said, smiling.

"Creeping critters," Ralphie whispered. "Why are they being so nice to us?"

"We want to be friends," Slime said, "so we're going to let you guys in on a secret."

Ralphie and Conrad were so impressed that the tough guys wanted to be their friends that they listened in awe.

"There are six jelly beans on the kitchen shelf outside Roachtown, next to the pink mug," Splat said.

"Six jelly beans!" Ralphie exclaimed, jumping up and down.

"But Ralphie, it's not even dark!" cried Conrad.

Spit, Slime and Splat sneered.

RALPHIE couldn't decide. The thought of the jelly beans was so tempting and he didn't want his new friends to think he was a coward.

"Come on, man, we're wasting valuable time here," Slime hissed.

"Don't listen to them, Ralphie!" cried Conrad, but Ralphie was already being led to the kitchen shelf with Slime's arms snugly around his shoulder.

"There they are!" Spit whispered, pointing to six huge jelly beans sparkling next to a chipped pink mug. "Look, red is strawberry, blue is blueberry, yellow is banana, pink is cotton candy, green is apple and orange is . . . orange. Now all you have to do is run over there, roll the jelly beans to the entrance and we'll carry them inside."

NERVOUSLY Ralphie crept out on the very tiptoes of his six legs and sneaked over to the first jelly bean. His heart was pounding. He began pushing the bright orange jelly bean. It was harder than he thought. He rolled and rolled until all of his legs were tired and finally he managed to move the juicy jelly bean close enough for Spit, Slime and Splat to grab it.

"Good going, dude," said Splat. "Only five more to go."

Ralphie was very tired, but he sighed and went back for another jelly bean. He pushed and pushed, and huffed and puffed.

H E was so tired that he didn't notice the kitchen door open and the Horribles walk in.

Spit, Slime and Splat took one look at each other and ran back to Roachtown as fast as their eighteen legs could carry them. Poor Ralphie didn't see Hedda Horrible's hand reaching for her favorite pink mug. As she picked it up, she noticed a yellow jelly bean moving on its own.

"Helmut, have you ever seen a moving jelly bean?" she yelled.

" ' Y o u silly old bat," Helmut said, looking over her shoulder, "don't you see there's a roach attached to it?"

"AAAEEAAAEEEAAH!!! Do something, Helmut!!" Hedda screamed.

At the sound of Hedda's scream Ralphie turned to see her horrible face looming above him. Ralphie had never seen a human face and this one was *so* close.

"Creeping critters, that's the ugliest thing I've ever seen!" he thought, as his little legs began to shake with fear. Helmut grabbed a rolled-up newspaper and tried to hit Ralphie.

BOOM! BOOM! BOOM! Helmut hit a plate and then a bowl. Ralphie heard blows landing all around him. Terrified and confused, he ran in circles around plates, glasses and cups, unable to find his way back home. Luckily for Ralphie, Helmut hit a tray of knives and forks, sending it crashing to the floor. Suddenly Ralphie saw the entrance to Roachtown and ran as fast as he could.

Helmut saw Ralphie running and raised his arm for the final, crunching blow. But as he brought his arm down with full force, he slipped on some old macaroni on the floor and hit Hedda on the head instead. Ralphie had found his way back home, but now the Horribles knew about Roachtown!

RALPHIE ran smack bang into Conrad. He could hardly speak he was so scared. Trembling, he told Conrad everything. They both knew Roachtown was in terrible trouble now.

Suddenly, Conrad said, "Remember learning in school that there are billions of roaches all over the world? Maybe we could ask some of them to help us."

Conrad told Ralphie about a book he once read called *Roachinson Crusoe*. It was about a roach who was stranded on a desert island. He wrote a message asking for help, stuck it in a bottle and threw it into the ocean. Some roaches from a nearby island found it and came to his rescue.

"How is that going to help us?" asked Ralphie glumly. "The river is too far away for us to go to."

"Yes, but I know where there is water!" exclaimed Conrad.

"Really? Well, I have a tiny bottle Mom and Dad found in the park. I was using it to collect Helmut's smelly old toenails, but this is much more important!" said Ralphie gleefully.

B EFORE they could say another word, they heard the loud wails of an ambulance siren. Peering from the door, they saw Hedda Horrible being carried out of the kitchen on a stretcher!

"Creeping critters," whispered Ralphie. "I guess old Helmut really knocked her out."

"Come on, Ralphie, we can send the note while they're at the hospital," Conrad said.

O n a piece of paper they wrote, "HELP! WE ARE IN BIG TROU-BLE!" and signed it, "THE ROACHES OF ROACHTOWN, SEC-OND SHELF ON THE RIGHT, THE HORRIBLES' HOUSE, NEW YORK CITY."

They emptied Ralphie's bottle and slipped the note inside. Quickly and quietly they carried the bottle to the Horribles' kitchen, climbed into the sink and dropped the bottle down the drain.

"Yippee, there it goes!" they shouted, and they hurried back to Roachtown.

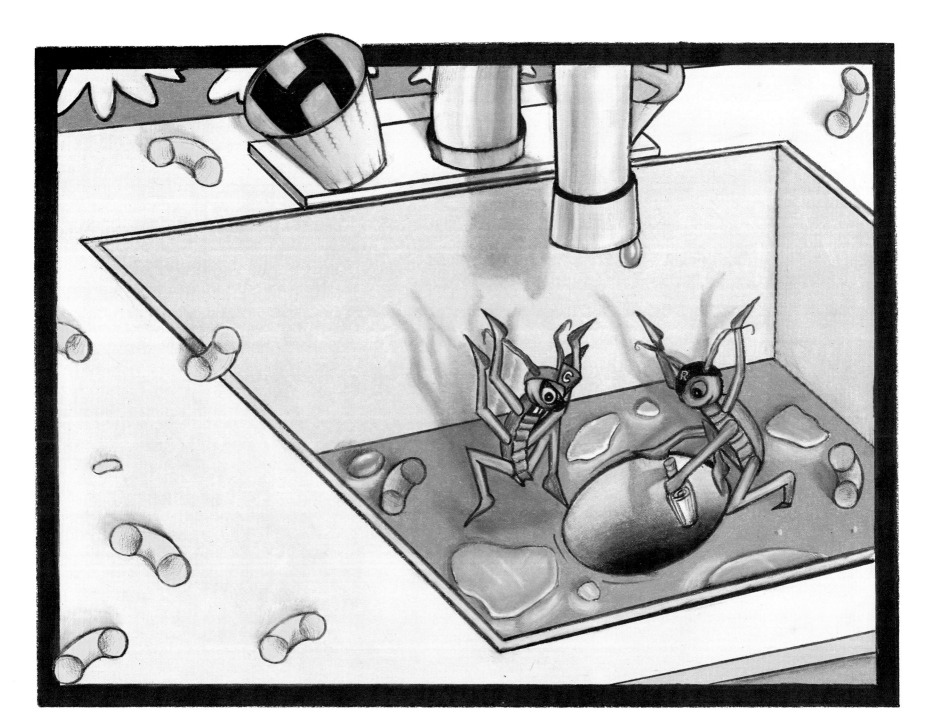

L A T E R that afternoon, Cuthbert Cockroach was on his way to work at the old post office by the river. He had walked the same path to work for the last twenty years and was in no hurry. His old legs were tired, so he stopped to watch the ships go by. As he looked at the river, he noticed a small bottle bobbing in the water. Curious, he pulled it out and uncorked it. To his surprise, it contained a note written by the roaches from Roachtown.

"Oh dear, I must help them," he muttered. "I know, I'll send a Morse code message through the telegraph at the post office!"

Cuthbert raced to work, feeling younger than he had in years. The post office was empty. All the PEOPLE had left for the day and, as usual, Cuthbert had the place to himself. But today he wasted no time and climbed on top of the desk containing the telegraph key. Hurriedly he jumped on it and began typing the message out in Morse code, sending it to every corner of the world.

B A C K in Roachtown, Ralphie wanted to tell his parents what had happened, but he was too frightened. He kept hoping that the Horribles would forget about him.

Ralphie and Conrad could barely sit still for the next couple of days and kept stealing out to the entrance to see if the Horribles were back. Their hearts sank on the third day when they heard Helmut's footsteps in the hallway.

"Creeping critters, we are in big trouble now!" Ralphie cried.

But Helmut had only come to pack a bag to stay with Hedda at the hospital. When he left, Ralphie looked at Conrad.

"I sure hope somebody finds our message soon," said Ralphie.

A T the end of the week, a big ship called *The Mary Roach* docked in the harbor across from Cuthbert's post office. On it were hundreds of thousands of roaches who had heard Cuthbert's S.O.S. Cockroaches from the entire world had gathered to help Roachtown. There were African roaches, English roaches, French and Italian roaches, German and Dutch roaches, lots of Russian roaches, Czechoslovakian and Swedish roaches, Spanish and South American roaches, Australian roaches, Indian roaches and even Japanese and Chinese roaches!

DURING the night, Cuthbert gathered all the roaches together and led them to the Horribles' house.

Ronald Roach was collecting crumbs in the park when he saw millions of roaches marching toward him.

"Have no fear, help is here!" Cuthbert shouted.

"What on earth are you talking about?" asked Ronald.

"Your urgent message for help, of course," Cuthbert replied.

"We'd better sort this out," Ronald said. "Follow me to Roach-town!"

As soon as Ralphie saw his dad and the millions of roaches behind him, he knew his message had been found and he had to explain. Ralphie's parents didn't even have time to scold him because they knew they had to work quickly. The Horribles could be back at any time now!

E A R L Y the next morning, the Horribles came home from the hospital.

"Helmut, you'd better get rid of all those disgusting roaches immediately," Hedda roared, "and make me a cup of coffee."

"Yes dear," Helmut said, as he pushed her wheelchair toward the kitchen. "I have some big cans of bug spray. We'll get that pesky little bug *and* his friends, or I promise we'll move!"

W H E N he opened the kitchen door, the Horribles could not believe their eyes. There were African roaches on the table, Russian roaches on the floor, South American roaches in the sink and French roaches on the wine rack. There were Italian roaches in the bread box and German roaches on the coffee machine. English roaches in the drawers and Swedish roaches in the refrigerator. Japanese roaches on the counter, Indian roaches on the stove, Spanish roaches on the shelves, Czechoslovakian roaches in the cookie jar and Chinese and Australian roaches on the chairs . . . The roaches of the world covered the entire kitchen!

''Eeeiiieeeiieeee!!'' Hedda screamed, falling out of her wheelchair. ''Get me out of here!''

''AAAEEEAAAAEEEEAAAH!!'' Helmut yelled, as he tripped over her. Picking himself up, he grabbed Hedda and pulled her out of the house. No one from Roachtown ever saw them again.

THAT night, the roaches held a huge party in the little old house which once again belonged to them. The Italian roaches sang, the Russian roaches danced and the roaches of Roachtown cheered! Everybody was happy . . . Ralphie most of all.